Noddy's Pet Chicken

HarperCollins *Children's Books*

It was a beautiful day in Toyland. Noddy and Big-Ears were going for a drive in Noddy's car.

"Thank you for giving me a ride in your car, Noddy," said Big-Ears.

"Yes, it's a great day to zip along," agreed Noddy. "*Zoom!*"

"Could you slow down a bit please, Noddy?"
asked Big-Ears.

Noddy was a little disappointed, he liked
to go fast.

"Thank you," said Big-Ears.

"Don't mention it. I care about others,"
Noddy said, proudly. "I listen when they tell me
what they want."

"Look!" cried Noddy, pointing to the middle of the road. "A chicken!"

Noddy and Big-Ears jumped out of the car.

"Are you lost, little chicken?" asked Big-Ears.

"I think he is," said Noddy. "Maybe I should take him home with me?"

Big-Ears was not so sure this was a good idea. "Are you sure a chicken would be happy living in your house, Noddy?" he asked.

"Of course," smiled Noddy. "I'll give him all my favourite foods and we'll play all my favourite games."

"You funny little Noddy," laughed Big-Ears.
"Well, he can have my seat in the car. I'm going to
walk. Good luck!"

"I don't need luck!" said Noddy. "I'm going to
treat this chicken very well."

Noddy was so happy about the chicken
that he sang a little song:

What a joy,
I'm a lucky boy,
Goody, goody,
Now I have a chicken.
He's my pet,
One I won't forget,
Yippee Skippee,
Now I have a chicken.

Noddy put the chicken in the car and began to
drive off very fast.

But the chicken didn't seem to like riding in
the car.

"Oh, dear, little chicken. What's wrong?" asked
Noddy. "Should I go slower?"

Noddy slowed down.

"But it will take forever to get back to town!"
sighed Noddy.

Noddy drove to the Ice Cream Parlour.
He bought two caramel treats. One for the
chicken and one for himself.

But the chicken didn't want to eat the
caramel treat.

"Go ahead, eat it!" Noddy said. "It's good!"

"Hello, Noddy!" It was Dinah Doll. "Who is your friend?"

"He's a chicken and I'm taking care of him. But I'm trying to give him a treat and he won't eat it." Noddy didn't understand. Caramel treats were his favourite sweets. Why didn't the chicken like them?

Dinah Doll had an idea. "Maybe he likes a different kind of treat."

Moments later the chicken was pecking away at corn from Dinah Doll's stall.

"Gosh!" exclaimed Noddy. "I didn't know chickens ate corn."

"Not everybody likes to eat the same things, Noddy," said Dinah.

"I'll remember that," promised Noddy. "Could I have some more corn for later please, Dinah?"

Noddy looked around Town Square. "What shall we do now, chicken?" he asked.

But before the chicken could answer, Noddy had already decided.

"I know," he said, running towards the tallest tree in Town Square. "Let's climb a tree!"

"Come on up!" Noddy called to the chicken.

But the chicken just stood there, looking up at Noddy. He didn't seem to want to climb the tree at all.

"Hmmm. I guess chickens don't like to climb trees either," thought Noddy. "Now what can we do?"

"Isn't this fun, chicken?" asked Noddy.

Noddy and the chicken were in Town Square with their roller skates on.

But the chicken didn't know how to skate.

"Should I give you a push?" offered Noddy.

Noddy was puzzled. The chicken didn't want
to eat any of Noddy's favourite foods or play
any of his favourite games.

"What *do* you want to do, chicken?"
Noddy wondered.

He thought about what everybody else
liked to do.

"If you were a cat you would like to
play with yarn."

"And if you were a dog you would like to play fetch. That's Bumpy Dog's favourite game."

Noddy threw a ball for the chicken.

"Fetch, chicken!" called Noddy. "I said *fetch*!"

But the chicken didn't want to play fetch either.

"Woof, woof!"

Suddenly, Bumpy Dog ran across Town Square.
He had seen Noddy throwing a ball and
wanted to play fetch.

"Bumpy, leave my chicken alone!" cried Noddy.

The poor chicken was very scared. He ran
towards the road.

"Stop in the name of Plod!" Mr Plod cried.

Bumpy Dog had chased the chicken towards Mr Plod.

Mr Plod didn't like chickens in Town Square.

"Noddy you can't have a chicken running around loose! Take it home," he ordered.

Noddy didn't know what to do. The chicken had not liked any of his games or his food.

Then Noddy saw Big-Ears and had an idea. "I know, I'll go and ask Big-Ears what he would do."

Later, Big-Ears listened to Noddy's story.

"But, Noddy," said Big-Ears. "All the things you wanted to do were PEOPLE things. Chickens like to do CHICKEN things."

"Golly, you are right Big-Ears," Noddy agreed. "I only thought about what I wanted to do."

"No wonder the chicken isn't happy," said Noddy, sadly.

Big-Ears looked at Noddy kindly.

"That's why I thought we should bring the chicken back to where we found it, Noddy. He might remember where he belongs."

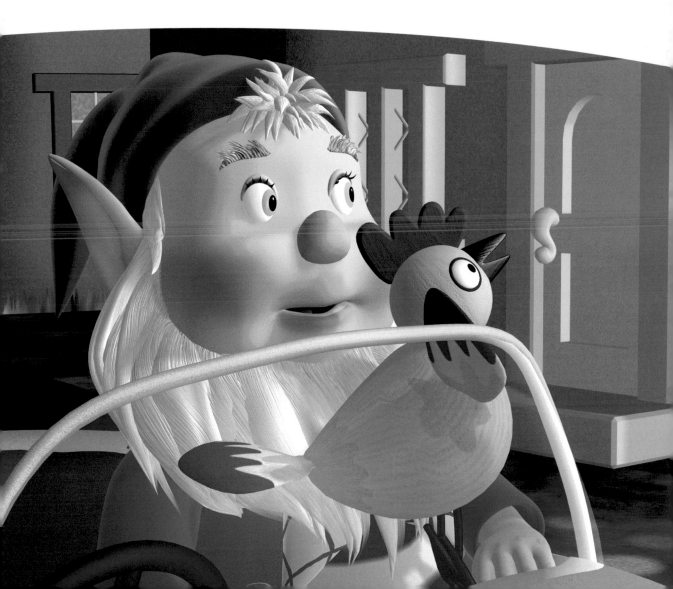

"Look, Noddy," cried Big-Ears. "The chicken
seems to recognise this street. Stop the car."

The chicken flew out of Noddy's car towards
a garden with a nice pink fence.

"Wait, chicken!" called Noddy. "What is it?"

"This must be his home," said Big-Ears.

"I don't want you to go, chicken," said Noddy.

"If you really want the chicken to be happy, Noddy, you will have to let him go home." Big-Ears knew Noddy would want to do the right thing.

Noddy lifted the chicken up towards the top of the fence.

"Yes, you're right, Big-Ears. I want what's best for him. Go home little chicken, I'll miss you."

The chicken flew out of Noddy's hands and over the fence.

"Noddy, you found my lost chicken!" cried
Tessie Bear.

Tessie Bear was standing on the other side of
the fence holding the chicken.

"He escaped two days ago. Thank you for
bringing him back."

"That's your chicken, Tessie Bear?" asked Noddy. "Why, of course it is. This is your garden, isn't it?"

"Yes," answered Tessie Bear. "Now I can feed him his corn and let him scratch in the garden. Those are his favourite things to do."

"So *that's* what chickens like to do!" Noddy said.
"The next time I find a lost chicken I will know
exactly what to do."

"Um, Tessie, could I come and visit the chicken
sometime?" asked Noddy, shyly.

"That would be lovely, Noddy," replied
Tessie Bear.

Noddy and Big-Ears waved goodbye to Tessie Bear and the chicken.

"Wow! Now I'm very happy I let that chicken go," said Noddy.

"So am I," smiled Big-Ears. "Things have turned out best for everybody."

First published in Great Britain by HarperCollins Children's Books in 2005
HarperCollins Children's Books is a division of HarperCollins Publishers Ltd,
77-85 Fulham Palace Road, Hammersmith, London W6 8JB

1 3 5 7 9 10 8 6 4 2

ISBN 0-00-721057-4

A CIP catalogue for this title is available from the British Library.

Printed and bound by
Printing Express Ltd, Hong Kong

make way for NODDY ™

Collect them all!

Noddy and the Treasure Map
ISBN 0-00-721056-6

Noddy Builds a Rocket Ship
ISBN 0-00-721058-2

Noddy's Pet Chicken
ISBN 0-00-721057-4

Goblins Above
ISBN 0-00-721059-0

Hold on to Your Hat, Noddy
ISBN 0 00 712243 8

Noddy and the New Taxi
ISBN 0 00 712239 X

The Magic Powder
ISBN 0 00 715101 2

Noddy's Perfect Gift
ISBN 0 00 712365 5

Bounce Alert in Toy Town
ISBN 0 00 715103 9

A Bike for Big-Ears
ISBN 0 00 715105 5

And send off for your free Noddy poster (rrp £3.99).
Simply collect 4 tokens and complete the coupon below.

Make Way For Noddy videos now available at all good retailers.

UNIVERSAL